Little Red Riding Hood

Illustrated by Courtney Autumn Martin

sequoia™
children's publishing

Once upon a time, there was a girl named Little Red Riding Hood. One day, Little Red Riding Hood's mother gave her a basket of bread and goodies. "Take this to Grandmother's house," she said.

Little Red Riding Hood gladly took the basket and skipped down the path.

Little Red Riding Hood was on the forest path when a wolf began to follow her.

"Good morning," said the wolf. "Where are you going this fine day?"

"I am going to my grandmother's house," answered Little Red Riding Hood.

"May I join you?" asked the wolf in a friendly voice.

Little Red Riding Hood knew she wasn't
supposed to talk to strangers, but she was happy
to have someone to walk with.

When she stopped to pick flowers, the wolf
sneaked away. It turns out this wolf wasn't a
friendly wolf at all—he was a hungry beast who
wanted to have Grandmother for dinner and
Little Red Riding Hood for dessert!

The wolf easily found Grandmother's house,
and pretended to be Little Red Riding Hood at
the door.

In his best little-girl voice he said,
"Grandmother, it's Little Red Riding Hood.
I brought you some goodies. May I come in?"

Grandmother could see the wolf from her window,
so she hid in her closet and
waited for the wolf to go away.
But the wolf didn't leave.

The wolf dressed in Grandmother's nightgown, bonnet, and glasses. Then he crawled into her bed and waited.

Little Red Riding Hood knocked softly. "Come in, my dear," answered the wolf.

Little Red Riding Hood noticed that Grandmother looked very strange.

"Grandmother, what big ears you have!" said Little Red Riding Hood.

"All the better to hear you with, my dear," answered the wolf.

"Grandmother, what big eyes you have!" said Little Red Riding Hood.

"All the better to see you with, my dear," answered the wolf.

"Grandmother, what big teeth you have!" said Little Red Riding Hood.

"All the better to EAT you with, my dear!" answered the wolf.

"Oh, no!" she cried.

Father heard Little Red Riding Hood's cry echo through the forest. He ran to the cottage and chased away the wolf!

Grandmother, Father, and Little Red Riding Hood ate their basket of goodies together. And Little Red Riding Hood promised to never, ever speak to strangers again.

The End

New Words

riding hood
(riding hoods)
A **riding hood** is a cloak (heavy cape with a hood) that you can wrap around yourself to keep warm. In the past, people wore them on cold days just like you wear a hooded jacket today.

wolf
(wolves)
A **wolf** is a large predator that can live almost anywhere, from the arctic to the desert. Wolves usually live far away from people. Unlike in the story, real wolves almost never view people as food, but they do eat farm animals. Because of this, people have hunted wolves, and there are not nearly as many of them as there used to be.

forest
(forests)
A **forest** is a wild area of woods. Wild forests used to be more common, with long stretches of them between towns. It was easy to get lost in the forest, and lots of animals lived there, including wolves and bears. Because of this, forests were viewed as scary and dangerous places.

echo
(echoes, echoed, echoing)
Echo is a word for sound bouncing back off an object. It sounds like someone is copying what you say. Echoes can bounce off of several objects to travel pretty far: "Father heard Little Red Riding Hood's cry echo through the forest."

beast
(beasts)
Beast is another word for an animal, usually a large or dangerous one. In fairy tales, a beast usually has human-like or magical qualities. The beast in this story is the wolf. It can talk, wears human clothing, and is as smart as a person.

bonnet
(bonnets)
A **bonnet** is a hat that is made of soft cloth and ties under the chin. People wore them to protect their hair from dirt and dust. Bonnets are not very common these days, and you might get a few funny looks if you wear one down the street.

goody
(goodies)
Goody is another word for candy, cake, or anything delicious and sweet. You get lots of goodies when you go trick-or-treating on Halloween.

❧❧❧ Story Discussion ❧❧❧

After you are done reading the story, think about what Little Red Riding Hood did when she knew something wasn't right. Be sure to look back at both the pictures and the words. Now it's time to answer these questions and talk about what the story means to you. After you read each question, choose the best word or think of your own.

1.) Look at the beginning of the story when Little Red Riding Hood met the wolf. What was her first reaction?

She was glad to see her friend.	She knew she shouldn't talk to strangers.
She was afraid.	Something else?

2.) What happened next?

She told the wolf to go away.	She was happy to have someone to walk with.
She went home to tell her parents.	Something else?

3.) What do you think she should have done?

Cried out for Father.	Given the wolf the wrong directions.
Run away as fast as she can.	Something else?

4.) Look back at when the wolf arrived at Grandma's house. What did he do next?

He went away when she didn't answer.	He pretended to be Little Red Riding Hood to trick Grandma.
He offered to mow her lawn.	Something else?

5.) Look back at the wolf in Grandma's clothes. How did Little Red Riding Hood feel when she saw him dressed as her Grandma?

She was suspicious about how Grandma looked.	She was relieved that Grandma was okay.
She was excited to eat some goodies.	Something else?

Forest Maze

Help Little Red Riding Hood find her way safely to Grandma's house.

Forest Friends

Little Red Riding Hood is doing some sightseeing on her walk through the forest. Can you help her find the animals shown here? Do you see any other animals?